LAST
CHANCE
FOR
FREEDOM

LAST
CHANCE
FOR
FREEDOM

Marcie Miller Stadelhofen

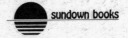 sundown books

New Readers Press • Syracuse, New York

ISBN 0-88336-206-6

© 1990
New Readers Press
Publishing Division of Laubach Literacy International
Box 131, Syracuse, New York 13210

Printed in the United States of America

Edited by Sheila Tucker
Revisions edited by Maria A. Collis
Illustrations by Chris Steenwerth
Cover design by Chris Steenwerth
Cover illustration by Michael Molinet

9 8 7 6 5 4 3 2

Table of Contents

Chapter 1

Gregory

Gregory sat on the dirt floor of the cellar. The owner of the Riverside Hotel had locked him in. At first, he tried to dig his way out. It couldn't be done, though. He would need a shovel.

Later, the cook brought him his lunch. In one hand, the man carried a gun. If he hadn't, Gregory could have pushed him right over and made for the river. So the gun was no surprise.

Still, Gregory wasn't used to this kind of treatment. Slaves get locked up often, but Gregory never had been. His master, Joel Rombey, had always trusted him. Mr. Rombey couldn't do without him, in fact. Gregory had become one of the best carpenters in western Virginia. He was good enough to earn money after work hours.

Soon, he would buy his freedom. You can't keep a good man down, slave or free. Gregory often told himself that, and Becky agreed. Becky was the prettiest and smartest girl around. He thought she loved him.

But that had been a week ago. Now, everything was different. These white people thought he was crazy. They kept him locked up. Becky had started the whole thing. She knew he'd buy her freedom, too, someday. But no, she couldn't wait. In fact, she lost her head. Her mistress wanted to trade her for another slave. Becky didn't even wait to see if her mistress meant to do it. She just ran away one night.

"I won't be here in the morning, Gregory." That's what she had said, but he hadn't believed her.

He should have gone, too. He had thought it was a wild idea. Well, staying at home was far worse. He and the master had left to look for her. They had got as far as the Ohio River. It was pretty certain she had gone across the river with a white man named Fairfield. He made a business of helping slaves escape. Now, she was in Ohio, on the freedom side of the river. Mr. Rombey could go over and look for her, though. He could even pay people to find her and bring her back. What he couldn't do was take Gregory to Ohio with him. If Gregory's own master brought him over to the freedom side, Gregory would be free by law. Instead, Mr. Rombey planned to send Gregory home to Mrs. Rombey.

"No!" shouted Gregory. "I'll swim across, if you don't take me with you." That was a stupid thing to say. Mr. Rombey told them to lock Gregory up at the hotel. Then, Mr. Rombey went off to Ohio.

When the cook brought him his supper, Gregory wouldn't eat it. He just lay there on the dirt floor. Whether he lived or died didn't matter, he thought. He got up, though, when Mr. Rombey came back. He still wanted to know about Becky.

"Come on, boy," the master said coldly. "You're going back to the shop."

"Did you find her?" asked Gregory.

"She got away again. Lord knows how. Someone saw her last night in a town just across the river," Mr. Rombey told him. "We thought she was with a family that hides runaway slaves. She wasn't there, though."

"Maybe she's in Canada by now," said Gregory.

"You don't know what you're talking about. Canada's not next door. She couldn't be there already. You can count on me, boy. I'll find her before she gets to Canada."

Gregory breathed hard. "I thought we were going back to the shop. What about those stalls you promised to finish at Hart's farm?"

"You'll get them finished, all right," Mr. Rombey told him. "If you don't, I'm through with you. You'll go south with the next slave trader. I don't know what's got into you."

Maybe you don't, Gregory thought. Maybe your head is bone straight through.

"You'll need the mule," Gregory said. "I'll start walking home."

"No, you won't!" said Mr. Rombey. "I'm not taking any chances with you. Abe Ryan is here with his partner. They'll drive you home."

Gregory said nothing. Mr. Rombey went out and found Abe Ryan. Next morning, they tied Gregory up in the bottom of Abe's wagon. Then, Mr. Rombey went back across the Ohio River.

Abe and his partner took turns driving their mule. It was a hot day. They were thirsty.

"He's tied up," Abe's partner said. "He can't get away. Do we have to die of thirst just because of old Rombey?"

"Don't you know he's crazy?" asked Abe. "Not Rombey, I mean, but him." He pointed at Gregory. "We can't leave him alone. He might set fire to the wagon. He'd probably talk all the slaves around here into murdering us."

"Well, he ought to be locked up, then. What's poor Mrs. Rombey going to do with him?"

"I don't know," said Abe. "Rombey told us to take him home. What she does with him is *her* lookout."

It was night when they reached the Rombey house. Mrs. Rombey came to the door with her lamp.

"Is that you, Abe Ryan? What's your business at this hour?" She didn't sound very happy.

"We brought you back your man slave. Mr. Rombey's over in Ohio, ma'am. He couldn't take Gregory with him. Fact is, the boy's gone crazy. We think you should lock him up."

"Gregory? No! He wouldn't ever go crazy. I can't lock him up. I need him to do the work." Gregory had sat up in the wagon. Mrs. Rombey held the lamp near his face. They stared at each other.

"He's not crazy," she said. "He's a bit too smart, if you ask me. I would never have bought him. It doesn't pay to have them too smart."

"No, ma'am," said Abe. "Well, if you think he's safe, ma'am, I'll be off home."

"He's safe," she said. "This one is staying right here. I'm not having any more runaway slaves. I'm not going to work myself to the bone."

Chapter 2

Mr. Rombey Foiled

Before he went to bed, Gregory had to chop wood for the stove. Next morning, he was out in the shop at five. They were behind in the work. There were chairs to finish. There were planks to prepare for the stalls at Hart's farm. Working with wood, Gregory forgot he was a slave. He forgot that Becky had left him. Mr. Rombey had taught him carpentry. But now, Gregory was better at it than the master. He was quicker, too. All the jobs would be done on time.

They would, if Mrs. Rombey gave him any peace. Soon, she made him come scrub the floor. Later, he had to clean the lamps. Most of Becky's chores fell to him. Mrs. Rombey had never done any work but sewing. Dishwater would spoil her hands, she said.

After dinner, Gregory washed the dishes. He was glad he didn't know how to cook. Mrs. Rombey didn't, either. Only she thought she was less likely to poison them than Gregory.

One rainy day, Mr. Rombey and the mule came, dripping, into the yard. The wagon was empty. Becky had got away. Mrs. Rombey said that she had never heard the likes of it. The girl was ungrateful. Mr. Rombey said she was worse than that. He did not want Gregory to hear the whole story. He sent Gregory out to give water to the mule. Gregory led the animal to a bucket already full. Then, he slipped back in the house and listened.

"You mean, she was on the boat you took to Detroit?" Mrs. Rombey couldn't believe it.

"Yes, but how could I tell it was Becky? She had on a silk dress. She kept her face veiled."

"You might have taken pains to find out. Her traveling all alone that way," said Mrs. Rombey.

"She wasn't alone," Mr. Rombey almost sobbed. "She had a maid and a white baby with her."

Mrs. Rombey gasped. "Did she steal the baby?"

"How would I know?" her husband asked. "She took it to Canada, anyhow. I watched her get on the boat for Windsor. She stayed on deck, by the railing. All of a sudden, she pulled her veil off. It was the first I knew she was black. And then, she yelled, 'Good-bye, Mr. Rombey. Don't look for me in Detroit. Say good-bye to Gregory for me.'"

Gregory tried not to laugh behind the door. For the first time in days, he felt good. He wished he could have seen Becky calling good-bye. Then, he remembered the mule and went out again.

Everything was changed now. Mr. Rombey had no confidence in Gregory. Gregory had no faith in Mr. Rombey. They worked side by side, but said little. Every time Mrs. Rombey wanted Gregory for chores, Mr. Rombey swore. He said if he ever found Becky, he'd whip her.

"She's in Canada now," Gregory reminded him.

"How do you know?" said his master. "Anyway, if she doesn't come back, you'll pay for her."

"How?" asked Gregory.

"With money you earn doing work for people after hours. You got eighty dollars already. Well, I'm taking half that money today. I had to pay your board in jail. I had to pay Abe Ryan to bring you home."

"That didn't cost you forty dollars," said Gregory.

"Maybe not. Just figure you're lucky to keep forty. What you earn belongs by law to me, boy."

Gregory didn't believe his master would take the money. He never had before. But, after work, Mr. Rombey said, "I want that money now. Go get it."

It was like a bad dream. Gregory didn't move. Mr. Rombey gave the order again, like a threat. Gregory could knock him down. Then, he could take the money and leave. He wouldn't get very far, though. They'd be after him in the woods with dogs. They'd shoot him or beat him half to death. He went, slowly, and got the money. Mr. Rombey took exactly half of it and gave the rest back. "If the girl isn't here in three weeks, you owe me all that. Then, you can earn ten dollars a month for me after hours."

"How will I have the time?" asked Gregory. "Mrs. Rombey keeps calling me for chores."

Mr. Rombey shrugged and went in to his supper. Gregory sat down on the wood pile.

"I'll be a slave till I die," he said out loud. He hated himself as much as Mr. Rombey. Why had he let this happen?

It was getting dark. Two or three stars shone in the sky. Gregory lay back on the wood and watched them.

All right, he *wouldn't* let it happen! He would find a chance to run away. He could run away now. The trouble was, they would know in half an hour. He could run away after they were asleep. They could still catch up with him in the morning. Dogs would find him in the woods. Becky got away because she had a white man helping her. No white man Gregory knew would help him. No black man *could* help him. He was on his own. He had to find some place to go quickly. And then, he remembered.

A year before, a strange man had stopped for repairs on his wagon. He called Gregory *thee*, as though they were in the Bible. He called Mr. Rombey *thee*, too. He even called them both *friend*. Mr. Rombey didn't like him. He said so to the next man who came to the shop. "It was that meddling Quaker," he told him. "He's dangerous. They say he wants a federal law against slavery."

Gregory had never heard again of the Quaker. Mr. Rombey kept books, though. He would have written down the man's name. What was it? Something to do with sheep. Wool—Wooler? No, Woolman. The Quaker's name was Woolman.

Did he have time to look at the books? How long had the Rombeys been at supper? He glanced toward the house. There was no sign of movement. He hurried through the shop toward the back room. Gregory could read a little. He thought he could find the name Woolman, all right.

It took a long time to find the right month, though. Every time Gregory heard a noise, he stepped back into the shop. Then, he had to find his place again in the book. There it was, at last: "May 12, 1858, repairs to wagon shaft for Joseph Woolman of Buckhannon, $12.00." Old Rombey had charged twice what it was worth. Gregory closed the book and ran out into the shop. Someone was coming.

"What's keeping you, boy?" It was Mrs. Rombey. "I want the dishes washed. Then, the kitchen floor's got to be scrubbed."

"I'm coming, ma'am."

Mr. Woolman lived in Buckhannon. That was south. No one would expect him to run away south, Gregory thought. He could get to Mr. Woolman's, all right. Afterwards, it would be up to God and the Quaker.

Chapter 3

Galloway

Gregory was ready to go when the right time came. Often, he had made deliveries for Mr. Rombey. He carried chairs or planks in the wagon. Sometimes he was gone all day. Now, he never went anywhere. His master didn't trust him anymore. Mr. Rombey made all the deliveries himself. Anyway, Mrs. Rombey might need Gregory for housework.

The days turned into weeks. Gregory began to feel frantic. Would he have to go at night? Winter would come before long. By waiting, he might freeze to death on the way to Canada.

One morning, Mr. Rombey said that he wanted the rest of Gregory's money. Three weeks had passed, and Becky hadn't come back.

"No," said Gregory slowly. "I'm keeping it." He was about to tell his master that he had buried it. What could Mr. Rombey do about it?

Gregory was surprised that Mr. Rombey didn't yell. He kept his temper. "The sheriff will see to that," he said. "I'll tell him you got forty dollars of mine. He'll make you give me the money."

Gregory knew that he meant it. He went and got the 40 dollars. Now, he had nothing left.

They had finished making a big desk for a lawyer in Galloway. That was the next town, only five miles away. Even so, Mr. Rombey planned to deliver the desk himself.

They loaded the wagon at evening. He would start early in the morning.

"Mind you don't scratch the top," he told Gregory. They were lifting the desk over the wagon tail. "Catch that drawer!" he yelled. "It's ready to fall."

Gregory held his end of the desk with one hand. With the other, he grabbed the drawer. Then, he laid it on top of the desk. But Mr. Rombey had lowered his end a few inches. The drawer skidded to his side. The corner of it whacked Mr. Rombey in the chest, pushing him backward. He dropped one leg of the desk on his left foot.

After that, Mr. Rombey lay on the ground cursing Gregory.

"Why didn't you say you were lowering your end?" Gregory asked. "How was I to know?" He helped his master up and brought him a chair. Mr. Rombey couldn't walk on his left foot. He said that his right lung could hardly hold any air. Gregory called Mrs. Rombey. Together, they got Mr. Rombey to bed.

Next morning, he could breathe all right, but his foot was swollen. He couldn't get a shoe on it. "I've got to drive that desk to Galloway," he moaned.

"You'll do no such thing," Mrs. Rombey told him. "You keep your foot up high. If you don't, it will go on swelling."

"I promised I'd bring it this morning."

"Then Gregory will take it," Mrs. Rombey decided. "He won't run off between here and Galloway."

Mr. Rombey moaned again. He gave in.

"You be back by noon," Mrs. Rombey told Gregory. "You hear me? No wasting your time in Galloway!"

"Master told Mr. Carlton we'd look at his roof beams," said Gregory. "You want me to make two trips to Galloway?"

"Can't he wait?" asked Mrs. Rombey.

"Carlton's in a hurry," said Mr. Rombey. "If you're going to send the boy, let him do that, too."

So that was that. Gregory would have six hours to drive to Galloway, leave the desk, and start for Buckhannon. By then, the Rombeys would begin to worry. It would take more than an hour to send word to Galloway, though. It would take hours more to start a search. Night would fall.

"Get going, boy," Mrs. Rombey told him. "When you come home, you sweep the floor of this shop. I declare, men would live like pigs, if we let them."

"I will, if I get here before dark," he promised.

"You better get here before dark. If not, I will know the reason why!"

"Yes, ma'am," Gregory said. He clucked at the mule and drove out of the yard. "I reckon you will, ma'am," he added softly.

In Galloway, he asked where Lawyer Stone lived. In 20 minutes, Gregory had delivered the desk. Stone tipped him, and he went away. The mule ate an apple, while Gregory thought. They'd be glad to buy the wagon at the livery stable. He could get his money back. It would be risky, though. Was it a worse risk to start for Canada without money? Maybe the Quaker was dead. Maybe he had moved away. If so, Gregory could hide himself and starve. No, he had to have money. It was too late in the year to walk to Canada. Too late to find food on trees and in the fields.

He drove the wagon to the livery stable.

"Hey, Gregory, when's your master going to fix these doors?"

"He wanted to fix them today," Gregory said. "His foot's swollen up. Missus says it's gangrene."

"Boy, I hope she's mistaken!"

"So do I," said Gregory. "Anyway, the doctor's got to operate. He wants a big fee. We don't have enough in the house. My master wants to sell his wagon."

"How's he going to manage without a wagon?"

"This is our old wagon," Gregory told him. "We built a bigger one a few months ago."

"How much does he want for this one?"

"Eighty dollars down. Fifty in a month."

"You must have heard wrong," the man said. "I ain't paying a hundred and thirty dollars for an old wagon. Sure, I'd like to help Mr. Rombey. He's an old friend, but—"

"I can't go back without the eighty dollars," Gregory moaned. "Doctor will let Master die."

The man stood silent. Gregory held his breath.

"That doctor must be a fool. He can trust Rombey. Sounds like he expects him to die. Maybe he thinks Mrs. Rombey won't pay him." The man had it all figured out.

"She wouldn't, if he didn't save Master," Gregory said.

"Well, I'll tell you what. I'll pay you eighty dollars down. Ninety is all I can afford, though. If your master doesn't want to sell his wagon for ninety, he can pay me back."

Gregory nodded. "Thank you, sir." When he had the 80 dollars, he remembered the mule. "I have to look at Mr. Carlton's roof. Can I leave the mule here for a few minutes?"

"Sure. Put her in the paddock."

Gregory mumbled good-bye to the mule. He would miss her. She would miss him. He tipped his hat to the stable owner. Then, he crossed the street and started south. All he had with him was in his pockets. A bundle would look suspicious. Never mind, it wasn't cold. He was walking toward a new life. Maybe he'd never see the Rombeys again. No matter what happened, he'd be free. He promised himself that he'd be free.

Chapter 4

Buckhannon

All afternoon, Gregory walked south. He stayed away from towns and villages. If anyone stopped him, he would have no papers. A slave was supposed to have a pass. It had to be signed by his master. Otherwise, any white man could arrest him.

When he had a choice of roads, Gregory chose the bad one. He hoped he wouldn't meet anyone. The worst would be to meet someone who knew him. What excuse could he give for being there? He had just put up a barn door, he would say. Then, he got lost. That's why he was walking south. What was the name of the farmer who owned the barn? He didn't know. Would anyone believe he was that stupid? "Well, where is your pass, boy?" they would ask. "My master forgot to give me one. He's in bed with a bad foot." That would never keep him out of trouble. "I'll walk fast and avoid talk," Gregory told himself.

The sun was going down. Gregory had walked all day. The few people he did pass hardly gave him a glance. They were in a big hurry, too. He promised himself he could have a rest in three miles. All he had eaten at noon was dry bread from his right pocket. Now, he took a crust from the left pocket and ate that. There were no more pockets and no more bread.

After a while, he thought he had walked three miles. He stopped and lay down in the woods. Just a short rest was all he could allow himself. He had to keep ahead of the slave-catchers and dogs. By now, the Rombeys and the people in Galloway knew he had run away. Only they would think he had taken the road north. What kind of a fool would run deeper into slave country? Gregory was that kind of a fool. He shivered. The night breeze felt cold on his sweaty skin. And then, he fell asleep.

He dreamed the owner of the livery stable was chasing him. They were running on a high, steep roof. Gregory began to slide. When he got to the edge, he jumped off. The jolt of hitting the ground woke him. He had to get going again. Mr. Rombey would never

rest till he caught him. Gregory reached for his shoes to put them on. Then, he heard a hissing noise. Something darted out of the left shoe. He felt a sharp pain in his hand.

It was a black night. The moon hadn't risen yet. He couldn't see his hand at all. Maybe a snake had bitten him. How could he tell? He would just have to walk till he found some light.

When the moon rose, Gregory guessed he was near Buckhannon. His hand had swollen. He told himself it was probably a spider sting. Nothing to worry about. Still, his head was beginning to ache. His feet hurt, too. Along the road, he caught sight of an old cabin. There was light glowing in the window. He stood still to think. It was better not to talk to anyone. Better to go on and try to find the Quaker.

Just then, the door of the cabin opened. A big black man stood in the opening, his back to the light. He was listening and looking. Gregory must have made more noise than he knew.

"'Evening," said Gregory. "I got bitten on my hand."

"'Morning, you mean," grumbled the older man. "Better show me your hand."

Gregory went into the cabin. It was almost bare, except for one table and one chair. He held out the swollen hand.

"I think it was a big spider," he said.

The man looked hard at it. "Snakebite, " he said. "You should have come sooner. Sit down." Then, he went to the corner and opened a big sack. He came back with a knife and a bottle. "Take a drink of this," he said. He uncorked the bottle.

"Is it a remedy for snakebite?" asked Gregory.

"It'll cure you or kill you," said the man. "Come on. You look strong enough to take it. I got to draw out that poison before it makes you sick."

Gregory drank a mouthful from the bottle. It tasted like bad whisky, and very strong. He kept his eyes off the man's knife. That didn't stop him feeling it, though. His head began to turn in circles. The man was drawing the poison out. When he finished, the man also took a drink from the bottle.

"You swallow some more, too," he ordered. "Then, go to sleep."

Gregory drank again and lay down on the floor. When he woke, he felt all right. The swelling in his hand was gone. So was the man who had cured him. Outside, it was not quite dark. Was it dawn? Could it possibly be evening again?

Gregory got up and went out the door. Rain was falling. He started on the road to Buckhannon. Pretty soon, he could see the lights of the town ahead. There was a man coming toward him. He was the old man from the cabin. He looked wetter even than Gregory. He acted tired out from a long day's work. If he saw Gregory, he didn't say so.

"Wait a minute," Gregory said. "Good morning. I'm all well again. Thanks for what you did. I guess you saved my life."

"'Evening," said the man. "You're welcome to your life." He was moving on.

"Just one more thing. I'm a stranger in Buckhannon. I've got to find Mr. Woolman. He's a Quaker gentleman. Do you know where he lives?"

The man turned around. He stared at Gregory for a moment in the dim light. "Maybe I do know," he said. "And maybe I don't want to stay mixed up with you."

"I'm not asking you to," Gregory said. "I'm asking you where Mr. Woolman lives."

"Man, who do you guess you're fooling? Think I can't tell you're a runaway? You talk enough about it in your sleep. I'm free, myself. I got troubles enough, though, in this county. I ain't sticking my neck out to help runaways. They'd have the law on me. They'd sell me into slavery."

Gregory said nothing. The man had done enough for him. He wouldn't get him into trouble. "Good-bye," he whispered.

"Just stay on this road into town," said the man. "Woolman lives two streets down to the left. A big white house without pillars. Now, get away from me. Don't ever mention you saw me."

"I promise," said Gregory. "Thanks for everything. I hope your troubles are over soon."

"Ain't likely," said the man, and that was all.

Chapter 5

Underground Railroad

Mrs. Woolman heard two short knocks on her door. It sounded like someone not sure he was welcome. She dropped her knitting on a chair and stood up. "Maybe another runaway slave," she muttered. "But we're not expecting any tonight."

She trotted over to the front door. Mrs. Woolman was short and plump and always in a hurry. All day long, she trotted happily from one event to another. An unexpected guest was a delight.

She opened the door. Rain was falling faster than ever. Blackness and the sound of water were all she recognized. Then, she saw a large man.

"Good evening," she said. "May I help thee?"

"Yes, ma'am. I'm looking for Mr. Woolman, please."

"Mr. Woolman will be home in an hour," she said. "Do come by the fire and dry thyself."

She gave a quick gasp when Gregory stepped into the hall. He was soaked from head to foot. Water poured from his clothes and his hair.

"Thee will want to change clothing. I'll get thee some. Come right into the kitchen."

In a few minutes, Gregory was dry again. He sat by the fire in Mrs. Woolman's parlor. She was making tea. The sudden warmth and comfort made him sleepy.

"I have never seen thee before," said Mrs. Woolman. "Are thee a traveler?"

"Yes," said Gregory. "I'm on my way to Canada."

"Ah, a railroad passenger, perhaps."

"No, ma'am," Gregory said. "I've never been on a train. I don't have money for the ticket."

"I am not talking about the Baltimore and Ohio line," said Mrs. Woolman. "Have thee never heard of the Underground Railroad?"

"No, ma'am. Where does it go?"

Mr. Woolman came in before his wife could answer. He remembered seeing Gregory at Mr. Rombey's place. He said he was glad to

see him. "Thee fixed my wagon shaft just right," he said.

"You paid for it," said Gregory. "I'm on my way to Canada. Can you help me at all?"

"Ah!" said Mr. Woolman, just as his wife had. "Perhaps we can help thee. We are stockholders in a railroad."

"Oh," said Gregory, "the one that runs underground?"

Mr. Woolman nodded. Supper was ready. Mrs. Woolman asked them to sit down at the table. They thanked God for Gregory's coming. Their guest looked at them in surprise. Gregory might well thank God for bringing him there. He couldn't see, though, why the Woolmans should feel thankful.

Gregory ate enough for three. He was a little embarrassed. But the ham and the creamed potatoes tasted so good, he couldn't stop. Mrs. Woolman kept offering him more.

"Where does your underground railroad leave from?" Gregory asked.

"There's a station right here."

"In Buckhannon?" asked Gregory. "What luck!"

"Thee might have got on a station or two sooner," Mr. Woolman told him.

"Not coming from Galloway," said Mrs. Woolman. "Our railroad only runs north."

Gregory began to feel troubled. "You must have to bring the cars back south. Your railroad will go bankrupt."

"I'll tell thee how it works," said Mr. Woolman. "Our customers mostly get to Canada, all right. Yet they do not often ride on tracks. Their road is not underground, either. Our passengers are all runaway slaves. We take no others. They vanish from their masters, as though they went underground. Then, they get carried from station to station. We have a wide network. Thee will go through Ohio and across Lake Erie. Others cross Pennsylvania or New York. Each conductor takes them as far as the next station. There, he turns them over to another conductor. I have never been a proud man. Yet I am proud to be a conductor."

Gregory still felt confused. "Why do you do it?" he asked. "Isn't there a thousand-dollar fine for helping slaves escape? And jail, too?"

"Yes, those are the risks," said Mr. Woolman. "But thee must have noticed something, friend Gregory. Where there is no risk, there is no prize to win."

"That's so," Gregory agreed. "I'll risk a lot because I want freedom. The prize will be mine, though. What will you ever get out of it?"

"We think God meant the world to be beautiful. We are tired of its ugliness. Can thee understand, Gregory? We want to see justice. We want to see all people free. Every time a friend reaches freedom, we have won a prize. We are nearer to making the world beautiful."

"Well," said Gregory, "if there were more people like you—"

"There are many like us. We couldn't have our railroad, if there weren't."

"Are a lot of them white men?" Gregory asked.

"A great many. A lot are blacks, and quite a few are mulattoes. Perhaps there are Chinese. I know there are Indians."

Gregory was amazed. "We should form an army. Then, we could attack the slave owners. We could free everybody at once."

Mr. Woolman disagreed. "Killing has never made the world beautiful. Killing never healed an ugly wound. That is not the way, Gregory. Armies spread death and suffering. They rarely bring justice and freedom, as well."

Gregory thought about it for a while. Then, Mrs. Woolman asked him if he didn't feel sleepy.

"It's safer to travel at night," he said. "If you tell me the way to the next station on your railroad—"

"No, don't go tonight," Mr. Woolman said. "Thee should sleep and keep dry. Tomorrow, I'll drive thee to the next station. Did thee know that I am a printer by trade? I have deliveries to make north of here. Thee can travel in my wagon. It has a special corner for a passenger. No one can see it from inside the wagon or out."

"Thank you, sir, and you, too, ma'am. You make me want to do something for the Railroad."

"Perhaps thee can, Gregory. Perhaps thee will."

Mrs. Woolman led Gregory to the spare bedroom. He slept soundly all night. At dawn, someone knocked on his door. Through the window, he saw that the rain had stopped.

Mrs. Woolman called him to the kitchen. Gregory had never eaten such a breakfast. Oatmeal, sausages, eggs, applesauce, biscuits, jam, and coffee. He ate and said good-bye to Mrs. Woolman.

The printer's wagon looked beautiful. Yes, he had repaired the shaft well. He hadn't known there was a secret hiding place inside. The wagon had glass-paned windows. In the back, books and papers were piled high. All the piles seemed to start on the floor. They didn't really, though. You began by moving eight or ten books from one pile. The large volume just under them turned out to be the top of a chest. You pulled it open. Inside, it was deep. A man could sit in it. He could lean back on pillows. Through one of the windows came light. The glass was painted over, though, to keep people from looking in. Still, he could open it enough to let in air.

Gregory got in. Mr. Woolman put the books back on top of the secret chest. Then, they started for the next station. It was Gregory's first ride on the Underground Railroad.

Chapter 6

Kingwood

It was a long day. The secret place in the wagon grew tiresome. If Gregory had walked all the night before, he could have slept. The trouble was, he did not feel tired. He wanted to see the country. The window, though, was painted over. He could only see a little of the road through the opening at the top. He wanted to talk to Mr. Woolman, too. They would have had to yell, though.

At noon, Mr. Woolman stopped in the woods. He fed and watered the horse. He and Gregory ate bread with cheese. The horse took an hour's rest. Gregory could walk a little. Then, they started on. They were moving north and a little east. Soon, they would be near the state of Maryland. From the highest place on the road, Mr. Woolman could see the mountains of Maryland. Gregory couldn't see, though. He wondered if anything looked different.

In the late afternoon, they came to Kingwood. The Underground Railroad had a station there. Kingwood lay in coal-mining country. The conductor who would carry Gregory on north was a miner.

The printer's wagon went straight through the town. They turned onto a bumpy, narrow road. It went down into a hollow. Then, the wagon stopped. Mr. Woolman got down from the seat. He opened a big door. Gregory stayed hidden till the wagon was inside a barn. Then, he got out and stretched his legs. There were no horses or cows in the barn. The beams didn't look safe. The building would soon fall down. Mr. Woolman said he'd never noticed that. Only a carpenter would be bothered by such things.

The house looked old, but more solid than the barn. A thin, tired-looking woman pointed at chairs in the kitchen. She brought them tea to drink. Mr. Woolman called her Mrs. Lane. She said very little. She seemed too discouraged.

After a while, Mr. Lane came home from the mine. Gregory could hardly guess what his normal color was. So much of his face and hands were smudged with coal.

"I wasn't expecting you, Woolman," he said. "I've been at work since four this morning."

"Then have thy supper and go to sleep, Bob." Mr. Woolman shook hands in spite of the coal dust. "My friend Gregory can wait. He has brought money to pay his board."

Bob Lane looked Gregory up and down. "He's big and tough," he said. "Makes me sick to see him run away. He ought to join up with John Brown."

"With John Brown? I heard he's gone to Canada, too," said Mr. Woolman. "Can he find work for Gregory there?"

"He has work for Gregory right here in Virginia. He's on a farm near Harpers Ferry. Been there all summer."

"Gregory's a carpenter," said Mr. Woolman. "He has never farmed. And he can't stay in Virginia. By tomorrow, he'll be advertised."

Bob Lane laughed. His voice filled the small kitchen. Nobody else could see what was funny. "You're as innocent as a baby, Woolman. Brown may be farming a little bit. No one knows he's Brown, of course. I know you won't tell anyone, though. And I can tell *you* that he's got more important business than farming."

Mr. Woolman frowned. "It's useless for us to argue, Bob. John Brown is a great man. He is violent, though. He has shed too much blood in the name of freedom, already. May God preserve Gregory from shedding blood!"

"It may come to that," said Bob. "Can't you see it's worth it, Woolman? To end slavery? Brown will make owning slaves unsafe. His men can keep stealing slaves till the owners give up. Maybe Brown's men won't kill anyone."

"Yet Brown killed in Kansas," said Mr. Woolman.

"Well, he ain't a Quaker," said Bob. "That's for sure. The slave owners kill, too. They killed Brown's son. Slavery is evil, Woolman."

"I know. But bloodshed leads to more bloodshed. Isn't it better work to heal than to kill?"

Bob Lane groaned. "You want to go to Canada?" he asked Gregory.

"I sure do," Gregory answered. Why should he get into a fight with slave owners? He wanted to find Becky. He wanted to be free.

"Then I'll start you north tomorrow night," Bob promised. "We can't all be heroes." He sighed.

Mr. Woolman said that he had to go. He had someone to see in the next town. He would spend the night at an inn. Gregory walked to the barn with him.

"I am troubled, Gregory," Mr. Woolman said. "I would not have brought thee here, had I known."

"I'll be all right," said Gregory. "Don't you worry. I have to take this railroad north."

"I might have found another route. But it's too late now. Be wise, Gregory. Use your freedom well."

Gregory said he would try. He would never forget the Woolmans.

Back in the house, Mrs. Lane had supper ready. Bob Lane had washed the coal from his face and hands. "Sit down, man," he said. "You're welcome here." They ate fried hominy grits and drank cider. Mrs. Lane did not sit down with them. Gregory thought it was because she wouldn't eat with a black man.

"I know what you're thinking," Bob said. "My wife doesn't ever sit down to meals, even with me. She doesn't like to talk. Not since she lost her father and brother in a mine accident."

"That must have been awful hard," said Gregory.

"Yes, she's been ailing ever since. She needs me. If she didn't, I'd go join John Brown."

"What's John Brown going to do?" asked Gregory.

"Free slaves, I told you. There won't be a slave left in Virginia six years from now. And when Virginia gives up, the other slave states will, too. The country will be free. You listen to me, Gregory. This is the biggest thing that's happened to this country in a long time. Biggest thing since they signed the Declaration of Independence."

"If it works," said Gregory.

"It ought to. Of course, it's dangerous. I won't push anyone who likes to stay safe."

"Safe?" said Gregory. "I don't care so much about being safe as being free."

"And what about other slaves? They want to be free, too."

Gregory thought about it. "If we all ran away, that would work, too."

Bob didn't agree. "It has to be organized. Most slaves are too scared. They don't know where to go." He told Gregory to think about it. Then, he went to bed.

Gregory did think about it, all the next day. It was Saturday. Bob only worked eight hours. When he came home, Gregory said, "I'll join Brown. I know Mr. Woolman wouldn't like it. Brown's way is the quickest, though, if it works."

"That's right," said Bob. "He'll save us all."

"How do I get to him?"

"I've borrowed a mule and a cart. I'll drive you part of the way."

Mrs. Lane gave them their supper early. It was the same as the night before. Outside, it was almost dark. They hitched the mule to the wagon.

Then, Gregory said good-bye to Mrs. Lane.

"Take care," she said. Those were the only words she ever spoke to him.

Chapter 7

Take Me to Harpers Ferry

"Hurry up, man," Bob called. "You have a train to catch."

Gregory got into the cart. "I thought this was my railroad," he said.

"It is, but you're not riding it far. You're going on the Baltimore and Ohio Railroad to Harpers Ferry. If you don't, you'll get there too late."

"Too late for what?" Gregory asked.

"You ask John Brown, when you meet him."

"Is there still time to catch the train?"

"I think so," said Bob. "There's another problem, though. How will you get on it?"

Gregory stared at Bob in the darkness. The question sounded stupid. You climbed steps to get on a train. But you had to buy a ticket first. "Guess I have enough money," he said.

"Listen, Gregory," Bob said. "They've already printed advertisements about you. I saw the ad in town. Your master's offering a big reward. Five hundred dollars! Everyone in Kingwood knows about it. Nine out of ten men on the street are out looking for you."

"We're already out of Kingwood," said Gregory.

Bob groaned. "You're advertised in every town in Virginia."

"I suppose so," said Gregory. "You mean I can't buy a ticket. They'd ask questions. Maybe you could buy it. Will they ask questions on the train?"

"Yes," said Bob. "They'd want to see your pass. You could say you are free. Then they'd want to see your papers proving it."

Gregory felt tired. "What's the use of going to the train, then?"

"I've got a friend who's fireman on this route. He could take you in the engine. I've sent him passengers before. You go to the engine and say 'Is this the train for Atlanta?' Then you listen to the fireman's answer. He should say 'Yes, by the long way 'round.' If he doesn't, don't argue. Just go away."

"You mean, your friend may not be there."

"That's right. He can't work every day and night," said Bob. "What I'll do is wait in the cart. I'll stop behind the station. If you don't come back, I'll know you're on the train."

"Or already in jail," said Gregory.

"You've got legs, man. If anyone bothers you, walk off. Run, if you have to. Jump in the cart before they see you."

It began to rain again. They spread the blanket over their shoulders. Still, it didn't keep their heads dry. After a while, they had to cross a small river. There was no bridge.

Crossing the river didn't take long. On the other side, Bob knew a farmer. Bob borrowed a horse from him. The mule could rest for a few hours.

"Now, we'll make good time," said Bob. "This is a lively horse. Listen to me, Gregory. I'll tell you how to find John Brown."

Gregory was thinking of Becky. If he missed the train, he would forget Brown. What was the use of being free, if you gave your life away?

"Are you listening, man?" asked Bob.

"Yes, I hear you. You say Brown doesn't use his own name. He's called Smith," said Gregory.

"Right. He and his men live on a farm in Maryland Heights. It's five or six miles north of Harpers Ferry. That's where you get off the train. Find the Potomac Bridge. Cross the river. When you're in Maryland Heights, ask where Smith's farm is. Have you got that straight?"

"Yes," said Gregory. "What will Brown's men do?"

"I met Brown a year ago," said Bob. "I'll never forget it. A man with a vision. He told me his plan. He and his men will hide in the mountains. They'll talk slaves into running from the plantations. The weak and the scared ones they'll send to Canada. The brave and the strong will stay with Brown. He will soon have an army. People in the North already give him money for arms. When there are enough men, they will raid the plantations. They will carry off food and free slaves. They won't fire on anyone who doesn't resist them. Then, the army will find new hiding places. They'll raid more plantations. No one will buy slaves anymore. No one will be able to keep them."

"No," said Gregory. "It will be the end of slavery. It ought to work. Why not?"

"It will," said Bob. "I met one of Brown's men last month. They're planning something new. There's an arsenal at Harpers Ferry."

"You mean the government keeps guns there?" asked Gregory.

"That's right. Brown and his men will attack it. There must be a hundred of them by now. They will get guns enough for everybody."

"I thought people in the North buy guns for them."

"No. I said that Northerners send money," Bob told him. "Buying arms is different. When you order a lot of guns, people suspect something."

"That must be true," said Gregory. He tried not to think of Mr. Woolman.

The horse cantered into a small town.

"This is where you take the train," said Bob. "You remember what you ask the fireman?"

Gregory did remember. Bob parked the cart behind the station. Then, they shook hands. Gregory set off around the corner of the depot.

The Baltimore train was ready to leave. Gregory ran toward the engine.

"Say, where are you going?" someone called. People would guess he was a runaway slave. He couldn't help it. The train started to move. Still, he ran harder. He was even with the engine. He leapt onto the step.

"Is this the train to Atlanta?" he shouted.

A startled face turned his way. "Do you have to scare people to death?"

Gregory looked at the ground. The train was gaining speed. He got ready to jump.

"Sure it is," said the fireman. "By the long way 'round. Come on in, before you fall off."

"Take me to Harpers Ferry, will you?" Gregory asked.

"Sure, if that's what you want. Any friend of Bob's can sit on my coal bucket."

Chapter 8

The Raid

Gregory sat on the coal bucket the rest of the night. He saw Harpers Ferry gray in the dawn. The engine chugged into the station. Then, it puffed and stood still. Gregory said good-bye and jumped to the ground. It was Sunday morning. No one was there to notice him.

The train was pulling out again. Gregory walked around the station house. Light glowed through a window. Inside, he saw a black man lighting the stove. Gregory opened the door.

"'Morning," said the man. "Better come over by this stove. You look cold."

"Thanks," said Gregory. "It's about as cold in this station as outdoors."

"Well, give the stove time, will you? It's been out all night."

Gregory nodded. "I can't stay, though. I came to ask where the Potomac Bridge is."

"That's easy. You just follow Potomac Street. We only got two streets in this town. I'll show you the right one. Have a cup of coffee."

"I'd better not," said Gregory. "Thanks, but I'm in a hurry."

"Oh," said the man. "You're on your way north."

"I've got an appointment in Maryland," Gregory told him.

The man nodded. "My name is Hayward Shepherd. I was born free, right in Harpers Ferry. Maybe I'll go north someday myself."

"If we don't freeze there," said Gregory, "it's a better life."

"What's your name?" Hayward Shepherd asked.

"Me? Just call me Adam. Adam Jones is my name."

"That's fine," said Hayward. "I'm relieved. They put up an ad yesterday for a runaway slave. He sounds a lot like you. His name isn't Jones, though. It's Greg something. If you meet him, tell him to stay away from towns."

"I'll remember," said Gregory. "Will you show me the way to the bridge now?"

Hayward went to the door and pointed. "Good luck," he said. "Maybe we'll meet again."

Gregory doubted it. He set off in a hurry. There was hardly anyone on the street so early in the morning. The watchman on the Potomac Bridge had fallen asleep.

Once on the other side of the river, he was in Maryland. Someone on horseback passed him. The man turned and looked back. He was white. He might have seen the ad for the runaway, Gregory thought. Suddenly, Gregory felt like running. He stopped himself just in time. That would be the stupidest thing he could do.

The man turned his horse and came back. "I'm on my way to Smith's farm. Know where that is?" he asked.

"I've heard of it," Gregory said.

"You've heard of it. Are you going there, too?"

"I heard it's in Maryland Heights. Know where that is?" asked Gregory.

The man nodded. "I'm going that way. You can follow, if you want to."

He never looked back again. But he slowed his horse down to a walk. Gregory followed. It was five miles uphill. Then, they turned onto a narrow road. It led to a white frame house. The horse stopped. The man got off.

"Is there someone you want to see here?"

"Mr. Smith," said Gregory.

"I guess he'll see you," the man said. Then, he led his horse to the barn. Gregory waited at the front door of the house. He didn't feel like knocking.

Suddenly, the door opened. A tall boy looked out. "Where's Cook?" he asked. "I saw him from the window."

"I guess he's in the barn," said Gregory. "Is Mr. Smith home?"

"Yes, he's here. I'll call him."

The man Gregory had followed came out of the barn. "Tell me who sent you," he said.

"Bob," said Gregory, "from Kingwood."

"Bob Lane sent you!" The man shook hands with Gregory. "I knew he'd get us some recruits. Come on in. My name is John Cook."

Gregory went into the house. The hall seemed dim at first. Someone was coming downstairs. Gregory strained his eyes. He knew it would be John Brown. Then, a tall, lean man faced him.

"This is Gregory, sir," said Cook. "He's joined."

The man's strange eyes stared at him. Gregory stared back. Brown's face was all eyes and white beard. He seemed to look deep down inside a person.

"Do you know what's ahead of you if you stay?" Brown asked.

"Yes," said Gregory. "I know."

"Go with him to the kitchen, Cook. Get him something to eat." Then, he turned and went out.

In the kitchen, Cook found bread and cheese.

"How do you know my name?" asked Gregory.

"I read an advertisement about you. Then, I saw you on the road. I wasn't sure, but you were heading north alone. You looked about twenty-four and smart. All the description fitted. Anyway, we want recruits."

"How many men have you got?" asked Gregory.

Cook sighed. "You're number twenty-two."

Gregory nodded. "You need me, then."

"Most of us are well trained," Cook said. "We've been drilling all summer. With twenty-two, we can do everything we need to."

"Bob said we'd take to the mountains," said Gregory. "We'd carry guns up from the arsenal. But, around here, there aren't many hiding places. Won't we get trapped?"

"That could happen," said Cook. "Some of the men think it will. I don't. We don't have to stay at the arsenal long. The state militia will be slow getting there. Federal troops will have to come from too far. The people in town can't fight. We'll send agents out to the plantations. The slaves will come in from all around. John Brown expects three or four hundred the first night."

After breakfast, Cook told Gregory to sleep. He wouldn't have time to sleep that night.

After sleeping a while, Gregory helped move supplies to an old school. He worked with Newby. Newby was a free black. He'd been with Brown and his men all summer.

"Why are you here?" he asked Gregory. "You're halfway to freedom. Why don't you move on?"

"Well, what about you?" asked Gregory. "You're free already."

"I'll tell you why," said Newby. "I've got as much to lose as anyone. But I've got more to gain. My wife and children are slaves. Their master is going to sell them south. We've got two so little they can't walk. No way my wife can run away. We can free her, though. We'll go to the plantation. We'll get her and my children. Even if I die, the others will do it."

"I'm one of the others," said Gregory.

"You're young," said Newby. "It's too bad."

The men had supper together. For the first time, Gregory saw all 22 of them. They seemed calm enough. No one swaggered. No one looked thrilled. Some seemed to think they were going to their deaths. They didn't cry about it, though.

Brown ordered them to march at eight o'clock that night. It was already dark. The sky was cloudy. They handed each man a Sharps rifle. Gregory had never held a gun before.

Three men stayed at the farm. Two by two, the others started down the road. John Brown drove a horse and wagon.

No one talked. There was the rumbling of the wagon. There was the rustle of dead leaves. That was all. They walked toward Harpers Ferry like men going to a burial.

The road curved. Now, they saw the lights of Harpers Ferry. Two men turned off the road to cut telegraph wires. The others moved on. They crossed the bridge. The watchman was awake now. Still, he didn't have time to move. They took him prisoner. Then, two men stayed to guard the bridge.

"Fifteen of us left," Gregory told himself. They went to the railroad bridge. Again, the watchman was taken. Two more stayed to patrol.

The guard at the arsenal gate stared at them in surprise. His mouth hung open. Someone grabbed his gun. John Brown walked in the door. The whole place was theirs.

"Not a shot fired!" Gregory told Newby. "Even Mr. Woolman couldn't mind this."

"We're not out of here yet," said Newby. "Keep your bullets in your gun."

Chapter 9

Carry the News

At the arsenal, the night was quiet. Gregory stood guard by the door. Everyone in town was asleep. Only three of Brown's men had stayed to keep watch. The others went to take the rifle factory. It was easy. They left three guards there. Then, the rest came back to the arsenal.

Gregory thought the work was done. They had only to wait for the slaves who were coming to join them. Then, they could go to the mountains. John Brown was not ready to rest, though. There was time to raid a plantation. They could free slaves. They could take prisoners to exchange for more slaves.

Brown led the raiders himself. Newby went with them. Gregory had no training. He was left with two other men to guard the arsenal.

At one in the morning, Brown and the other raiders were not back. Gregory heard an engine whistle. An express train roared down the tracks. It was on its way to Baltimore. The engine stopped at the station for a few minutes. Then, Gregory heard it gasp into motion. It was heading for the railroad bridge. The guards Brown had left on the bridge had only to hide until the train passed. But the train stopped again. Gregory felt suddenly cold. For a moment, the night was silent. Then, a voice from the train called out, "What's that blocking the track?"

Next, Gregory heard footsteps on the tracks. A couple of men must have gotten off the train to clear the track, he thought.

"Keep still," Gregory whispered, as though the guards on the railroad bridge could hear him. "Don't panic. In a minute, they'll clear the track and go on." But then, he heard two shots ring out, and he knew that the guards had fired at the men from the train.

"That's it!" he told himself. "Anyhow, it's better than dying a slave." He walked down to the arsenal gate. Lights shone in the train window. The engine stood halfway over the bridge.

A man came running out of the station. He clattered down the street to the bridge. Gregory saw him in the light of a street lamp. It was Hayward Shepherd.

"Hey!" Gregory shouted. "Stay off the bridge!"

But Hayward didn't hear. Now, his feet were pounding on wood. A guard shouted, "Halt, there!"

"Where's the night watchman?" Hayward called. Hayward didn't halt. He kept running. There was another shot. The pounding of Hayward's feet stopped.

"You jackasses!" Gregory almost sobbed with rage. "Why? Why did you do that?" He

ran down the street to the bridge. "Don't shoot!" he yelled. "I'm coming to get Hayward. That was Hayward Shepherd you shot. What was the use?"

One of the guards pointed his gun at Gregory. He was so scared, he might shoot anyone. The other guard stopped him.

"Who the hell is Hayward Shepherd?" he asked. "Why didn't he halt?"

"He works at the station," said Gregory. "He was looking for the night watchman. He said so. Don't you have ears?"

"He's bleeding something awful," said the scared guard. "Better take him away."

"Put on a tourniquet or something," said the other.

"We'll move him into the arsenal," Gregory told them. "Come on. It will take three of us."

"One of us has to guard this train. You two take him. You can manage."

All together, they lifted Hayward. Then, Gregory and the scared guard carried him away. They laid him on the arsenal floor. Gregory saw that no tourniquet could save him.

"Is there a doctor around here?" he asked.

"Just two houses up the street," the guard said. "You can't call a doctor, though. The whole town would know." Then, he went back to the bridge.

Gregory ran out the gate and past the first house. The second door had the doctor's name on it. He knocked hard.

Someone opened a second-story window. A head wearing a nightcap looked out. "What's going on there? Who's been shot?"

"Are you Doctor Pate?" Gregory asked. "Hayward Shepherd got shot. Can you come right away?"

The doctor grumbled. It didn't take him long to come, though. "There's always some trigger-happy fool," he said. "Drunk, I suppose."

Gregory didn't answer. He led the doctor through the arsenal gate.

"What's Hayward doing here?" the man asked. Gregory shrugged. Doctor Pate knelt down and opened his bag. After a while, he asked, "Who shot him? It wasn't you, I guess."

"No. I'm not sure who it was. You're not going to give up, are you?"

"I'm trying to keep him alive, if that's what you mean. I should have stayed in bed. I would have done as much good."

Hayward never became conscious again. About four o'clock, the doctor said it was over. He packed his bag and started toward the door.

"It's locked," said Gregory. "Listen."

Up the street he could hear the sound of hoofs. It must be Brown and his men. Soon, they were banging on the door. Gregory hurried to open it.

John Brown came in first. He knew the doctor by sight. He said good morning politely.

"Hayward Shepherd from the station got shot," said Gregory.

"And you called Doctor Pate?"

"Yes, I couldn't let him bleed to death. He died anyway, though." Brown looked down sadly at Hayward's body.

"I'd like to go home now," the doctor said.

"Of course," said Brown. "Thank you, doctor. Good night." Gregory let him out.

"Why did the train stop?" Brown asked.

"The rail was blocked," Gregory said.

Brown shook his head. "So now, the train is late. They must have raised an alarm farther down the line by now. They've probably tried to telegraph, too. So they know the telegraph isn't working. Next, they'll send a messenger."

"Can't we move to the mountains, sir?"

"The sooner the better," said Brown. "Not yet, though. We'll tell them to let the train go. No use holding it any longer."

"Won't it carry the news faster? You can delay a messenger. You can't stop the people on the train from talking."

Brown smiled and shook his head. "We have time, Gregory, for whatever happens. We will have done our work if we live. We will have done our work if we die."

"Which work, sir?" Gregory asked.

"Isn't it our goal to free all slaves?"

"Yes," said Gregory, "but we haven't yet."

"Whatever happens here will lead to that freedom. Someday, you'll see." Brown turned and walked out. Gregory shook his head. Years would pass before he understood that Brown had changed history.

The arsenal was in an uproar now. Brown and his men had brought back three prisoners. They were owners of plantations with slaves. Ten of their slaves had come, too.

Gregory was sent to the schoolhouse in Maryland. "Tell Cook to bring his men," said Brown. "After that, go to the rifle factory. Carry the news to our guards. In a few hours, we leave here. We will pass their way."

Gregory asked for a mule. Then, he set off. For the third time, he crossed the Potomac Bridge. The train had gone before him. He could see it below, steaming toward Baltimore.

Dawn had turned the sky gray when he reached the schoolhouse. John Cook looked strained and tired.

"I'm glad we're ready to move," he said. "We haven't got half the recruits I expected. These days, everyone's scared. I'll wait an hour for late arrivals. Then, we'll start down."

From the valley came a clanging. Church bells were ringing.

"That's an alarm," said Cook. "The town knows about us now. They'll all be out in the streets. Next thing, the militia will come."

"How will they send for it?" asked Gregory. "You cut the telegraph wire. Remember?" He was really thinking about the train, though. Its passengers must already be spreading the news.

"I've got to go now," Gregory said. He crossed the bridge again. The town had come alive. Small groups of men stood talking on the street. They were waiting.

Gregory rode up the Shenandoah River to the rifle factory. The men there were eating breakfast. Smells of coffee and wood smoke made him feel weak. They gave him hot corn bread and scalding coffee.

Soon, he had to start back. He had given Brown's message. The mule carried him down to Harpers Ferry. Now, the whole town was in an uproar. Shots rang down the street. Brown's men no longer guarded the railroad bridge. Some of the townspeople had taken it. Gregory got off the mule. He let it go free. He tried to sneak through the town.

"Where do you think you're going?" a fat man asked him.

"I'm on my way home," said Gregory. "I've been away overnight."

"Have you?" said the man. "Keep your eye on him, Dick. See where he goes."

Dick was a big, sulky-looking boy about 17. He squinted at Gregory.

"Never saw you before," he said.

"I haven't lived here long," said Gregory.

"I bet not," said Dick. "I bet you're the slave on the ad over there."

"Ask Judge Perkins, Dick," the other man said. "Maybe you'll get a reward. Judge will know."

Chapter 10

John Brown, Good-bye

Then, the trouble began. Dick grabbed Gregory's arm. Gregory flung the boy off fiercely. He ran at top speed toward the arsenal. There was no time to think. He was sure that John Brown would be taken. If he went back to Brown, Gregory would surely die. Well, he would rather die with Brown than die a slave.

He zigzagged through the crowd in the street. Dick ran after him, yelling and cursing. At first, people tried to get out of Gregory's way. Then, they listened to Dick. They moved to block Gregory. One man even tried to trip him up. Gregory was almost at the arsenal gate. He was starting to yell, "Hey, let me in!"

But the yell turned to a cry of pain. One of the men had drawn a pistol. When Gregory wouldn't stop, he shot him. The man didn't try to kill Gregory. A strong, young slave was valuable property. That's why the pistol was aimed at his foot.

Gregory fell on his face. His heel bone was broken. He got on his knees at once and tried to crawl. It did no good. Dick was there, kicking him, before he got to the gate. Several men helped to drag Gregory back off the street. They tied his arms and legs.

Gregory lay on the sidewalk all afternoon. Sometimes, he even slept. He got used to noise and crowds. The pain in his foot was a dull ache. The heel had swollen to twice its size.

Gregory woke to a new uproar. Around him, people were rushing and yelling. He could hear rifles firing. Then came screams of pain. The townspeople were having a battle with Brown's men. It went on for 10 or 15 minutes.

The wounded and the dead were laid near Gregory. He lifted his head to look at each one. Three of them he didn't know. Then, someone shot Newby at the gate. They dropped him on the sidewalk. He was dead already. Gregory cried out in rage. Newby had gambled his life on this raid. He thought that enough of Brown's men would live to save his family. Gregory saw now that they didn't have a chance. He fell back, broken and half dead himself.

A troop of volunteers arrived from other towns. They broke through the arsenal gate. Then, they attacked the guards at the door. Brown and his few men had to escape by a back way. They took their prisoners with them. Then, they shut themselves up in a small engine house. The men from the town surrounded it as fast as they could.

"The army will get here tonight," a man said. "They'll open up that engine house."

It began to turn dark. Dick got the judge to question Gregory. It was no use. Gregory wouldn't say a word. He didn't care anymore. They asked him if he was with the men who took the arsenal. He just closed his eyes and tried to sleep.

"Put him in jail," the judge said. "We'll see about him tomorrow."

The jailer was a kind man. He looked at Gregory's foot. He said he would send for a doctor. Gregory said no, just leave him alone.

The jailer shrugged his shoulders. He brought Gregory soup and locked him up. There was another man in the same cell. He said he had stolen a horse. Now, he was waiting for trial. In the night, Gregory moaned so, the other man couldn't sleep. He got up and looked at the wounded foot.

"Better let me take the bullet out. You won't ever get well like that."

Gregory knew it. He said he didn't care. The foot throbbed more and more. It wouldn't stop swelling. It didn't even look like a foot anymore. At five in the morning, the jailer came back. Gregory was raving. He didn't know where he was anymore. He kept yelling to Newby to hide.

After they took the bullet out, Gregory grew quiet. He even fell asleep. When he woke, he heard the sound of shots.

The jailer said that the army had come. Colonel Lee was entering the engine house. He would arrest all the raiders. They would be tried and hanged. Gregory turned his face to the wall. There would never be an end to slavery.

Days passed. When they asked Gregory questions, he still wouldn't answer. At last, the judge made up his mind. Gregory was not one of John Brown's men. Perhaps the judge wanted Dick to get the reward. If Gregory got hanged, there would be no reward. The judge wrote to Mr. Rombey. Rombey sent one of his neighbors to Harpers Ferry. The man came to the jail. He knew Gregory at once.

"I got to find you a new owner," he said. "Your master never wants to set eyes on you again." Gregory looked through him like air.

The judge helped find his new owner. Near Harpers Ferry, a farmer was looking for a carpenter. His name was Sill. His son was getting married. Sill had to build a new house. Usually, he didn't keep slaves. This would save him money, though. He could buy a good carpenter. He could make him build the house. Then, he could sell him south.

They needed slaves badly there. Sill might even get a better price than he had paid.

"So don't think you're staying in Virginia. If you wanted that, you shouldn't have run away. You'll be going down to Mississippi. Or maybe Texas. Slaves don't run away from there."

Gregory said he didn't care about Virginia. Farmer Sill looked surprised. Then, they climbed onto the wagon seat. Sill drove out of town.

The road looked like one near Rombey's place. Every week, Gregory had driven along it. Once, Becky had come running toward him. He had helped her onto the wagon. Then, she had told him she was going to run away. He could have gone with her.

Farmer Sill stared at him. "You got something the matter with you?"

Gregory shook his head.

"I want you to build a house for me. You better be as good as your reputation. I paid a hell of a lot for you," Sill said.

Gregory nodded. Just one thing was sure. He would never go to Mississippi or Texas.

Chapter 11

This Side of Freedom

Becky washed dishes at the Hotel Canada. She was free now. She would never be a slave again. She earned her own living, too. In Windsor, Ontario, she had found her father. He wanted her to live with him. The trouble was, he had a new wife. Becky loved the dear, old man. She didn't love her stepmother. Patsy was her name, and she was bossy. So Becky only went home every other Sunday. The hotel gave her a room. It was up in the attic and cold as the North Pole. Today was November 17. Yet, in Ontario, it was already snowing.

Dishwashers have plenty of time to think. Becky wondered if she had done the right thing. Yes, she was glad she had run away. Cold didn't matter. Still, she had to admit that she was lonely. The people at the hotel were nice to her. She had even found other runaway slaves. They had their own friends and families, though. She was the only one she knew who lived alone. Well, that was the price she paid. But it didn't really need to be. Gregory could have come with her.

When she thought of Gregory, Becky almost stopped work. The plate she was washing sank back in the suds. Why had he been so cocksure of himself? He didn't want her to run away. He was going to buy his freedom. Then, he would buy hers. Well, she hadn't been able to wait. Her father sent her money to escape. Maybe if Gregory bought his freedom—but he couldn't do it now. Something had gone wrong. It was three weeks since the letter had come. Her friend Ruby had sent it. Ruby said Gregory had run away. There were ads for him all over western Virginia.

Becky had walked on air that day. She felt sure Gregory would come to her. She thought he'd arrive the next day, maybe. He'd at least come the next week.

He hadn't, though. Why did it take so long? Maybe he lost his money. Maybe he had to walk across Ohio. Then, he would have to stow away on a boat. He had even had time for that now. No, either Gregory had got

caught or he had gone to another place. Maybe he met a pretty girl in Detroit.

Becky could forget about him, she thought. Only he was hard to forget. She tried now to think about the glasses she was washing. She didn't really need Gregory. She could support herself. She was learning to read and write, too. Her teacher was named Barbara. Barbara had also been a slave in Virginia. She had run away years ago. She was a good teacher. Before long, Becky would be able to read.

Becky would never teach, though. She wanted to help slaves get into Canada. That's what Barbara's husband, Romulus, did. He owned a boat on the Great Lakes. Almost every time he came into port, he brought a runaway with him.

"I'll have enough to do," Becky told herself. "Don't need any man to look after." Anyway, there was always Hamilton, if she changed her mind. Hamilton was Romulus's partner. He didn't know much about steam engines. Sometimes, though, he sailed as first mate. Hamilton was rich, and he was handsome. Hamilton had seen Becky three times. Three times, he had asked her to marry him.

It was late when she finished washing the last dish. She couldn't go to her room, though. She had promised to stay with Barbara's little girl. Barbara taught a class of dock workers Monday nights. They were learning arithmetic.

"You look worn out," Barbara told her. "Here, sit down. I found a nice, easy book for you."

Becky said thanks, and Barbara left.

The little girl was asleep. Becky sat in an armchair and started the book. Yes, she could read it. She understood it all. There was hardly a word she couldn't get.

"I can read," she told herself with pride. "What do I care about Hamilton, or Gregory, either?"

Soon, Barbara would be back. Becky felt sleepy. Someone was opening the door with a key.

"Is that you, Barbara?"

The door swung open. It was Romulus, Barbara's husband. His boat was just in from Chicago.

"Hello, Becky," he said. "Is Barbara teaching?"

"Yes," said Becky. "Did you bring anyone with you this time?"

Romulus laid down his sack. He took off his coat. "You were expecting someone, weren't you?"

"Kind of," she said.

"Well, all I've brought back is news. It's not all good, either. A few days ago, we stopped at Cleveland. A white man asked for me. His name is Fairfield."

"Oh," said Becky. "He helped me escape."

"I know," Romulus told her. "He said a friend of yours named Gregory ran away."

"I heard that," said Becky.

"Well, he got caught. He didn't even get out of Virginia. Your old master just sold him to a farmer."

Becky refused to cry. She didn't dare speak. She knew her voice would shake.

"It's queer he went to Harpers Ferry," Romulus said. "Why didn't he come straight north? You heard what happened at Harpers Ferry?"

"Isn't that where John Brown made his raid? You think Gregory went with him?"

"I guess not," said Romulus. "He'd be in prison now. Be glad he's not. He's safe on some farm."

"Safe!" said Becky. "Anyone can tell that *you* were never a slave. Slaves aren't ever safe. They can get sold south any day. They can get beaten to death by an overseer. They can—"

"Don't cry, Becky." Romulus patted her on the shoulder. "That's why Fairfield came to me. He thinks we might arrange an escape."

"I don't have any money to pay Mr. Fairfield."

"He said he'd do it cheap. He wants me to bring Gregory across the lake. We'll all chip in. Fairfield says he'll do it without profit. We just have to pay his and Gregory's expenses."

"I don't know how to thank you, Romulus," Becky said.

"Well, don't then. I have something for you. I almost forgot. Hamilton stayed on in Detroit. He got invited to a party there. So he wrote you this letter. Here it is."

Becky took the letter and said good-bye. She was thinking about Gregory in slavery again. Gregory was killing himself at work on some farm. Mr. Fairfield would free him, though. He just had to!

Up in her room, she lit a candle. She read Hamilton's letter. "Hello, Beautiful. I can't make it back Tuesday like I told you. Big business deal in Detroit. I'll be back Friday, for sure. Marry me soon and live with your loving Hamilton."

Becky went to bed, still thinking of Gregory.

Chapter 12

Fairfield

"You really know how to build!" Farmer Sill was glad. He knew he had made a good deal. At first, he had doubted it. This man, Gregory, didn't sulk exactly. He just never said anything. He never smiled or laughed, either. Sill felt sure he was stupid and maybe dangerous. Half-wits should be little and harmless. This one wasn't.

Gregory was trained as a carpenter, though. On the farm, Sill showed him his drawing. He had made a plan of the new house. It was rough, but clear. Gregory stared at it for a few minutes. He couldn't help but feel interested.

"You can't build it this way," he finally said.

"What you talking about, boy?" Mr. Sill stared at him, his eyes popping.

"Roof won't hold up. You haven't given it enough support."

"You don't know what you're talking about," said Sill. It's one thing for a slave to be dumb. It's another for him to get bossy.

Gregory tapped the faulty roof with his finger. "You could put a post in here," he said. "Wouldn't look nice, though. I'd change the proportions."

Mr. Sill looked hard at the plan. Maybe Gregory was right. He set Gregory to work digging a cellar hole. Then, Sill walked over to the next farm. His neighbor knew a little about building.

When he came home, he had respect for Gregory's judgment. Sill didn't like being told he was wrong. But he was willing to listen.

The house was going up fast. Gregory enjoyed it. Someday, in Canada, he hoped to build one like it. At night, though, he had time to think. He could never get to Canada. Well, Farmer Sill had a gun. When the house was done, Gregory would use it.

Mr. Sill treated Gregory well. "You're going to make me a big profit," he said. "They'll pay a lot for you in Mississippi!" Gregory nodded. There was a queer look about his mouth, though.

The weather got cold. The work went on. One day, a white man stood watching. He must have stayed 10 minutes. Gregory thought he wanted a job. Mr. Sill wasn't there, though. Two slaves from a nearby farm were helping Gregory. Finally, the man went away. Later, he strolled past again. This time, Mr. Sill was there. The man didn't stop. He hardly gave them a look.

Gregory worked late that day. He was putting in windows. It was almost night, so he had to use a lantern. When he finished, he locked the door. Then, he started toward the road. The wind whistled. There was no moon. Maybe it would snow.

A voice wafted out of a roadside elm tree. "You, Gregory, stop a minute. I got news for you."

He had heard of ghosts caught in trees. He had never believed in them. Still, he shivered.

"Who are you?" he asked. "Come out where I can see you." Something moved from behind the elm. After a moment, he saw it was the same stranger.

"I'm John Fairfield," he said. "Ever heard of me?"

"I sure have," said Gregory. "You carried my girl off. You're the reason I'm here today."

"Well, why didn't you come with us?"

"Did she get to Canada all right?" Gregory asked. "What's she doing now?"

"She's doing well enough. She wrote you this letter. Can you read?"

"Becky wrote me a letter? Since when does she know how to write? I guess I can read it. I'll go back and light my lantern."

"Be quick about it, then," said Fairfield.

Gregory was not quick. He went in the new house and lit the lantern. Then, he stared at the letter. How did he know it came from Becky? He couldn't recognize her handwriting. She had never written before. Yet he was sure it was hers. The writing was the way she would have written. It stood up big and clear. He could read it.

Dear Gregory,
   This is my first letter. So pardon
the mistakes. We heard the bad news,
but don't worry. Mr. Fairfield says he
can take you to Lake Erie. My friend
Romulus is captain of a boat. He will
carry you to Canada. Pa and I are
well. Maybe we will see you in
Windsor, Ontario. Good luck.

                     Becky

Gregory felt drunk with joy. Becky had found him. He would be free. He would live with her in Canada. This man, Fairfield, knew how to manage his escape. Yes, but for how much? Becky might think he still had money. Fairfield, too.

He blew out the lamp and locked the door again. He went back to the elm tree.

"I read the letter," he said. "How much are you charging for this?"

"Your expenses have all been paid. Don't worry."

Gregory nodded. First, he wanted to cry with relief. Then, he hated himself for being helpless. He had hoped to buy Becky's freedom. Now, *she* was paying for *his* escape. Or was this friend of hers, Romulus, paying? That would be worse. Gregory wasn't the man he had been. She wouldn't marry him. She could even write now, and he couldn't. The letter said "*maybe* we'll see you."

"Here's what you've got to do," said Fairfield. "Can you get out of the house at night?"

"Not till early morning. Mr. Sill goes out to do the milking before light. I go, too, to get wood for the kitchen fire."

"How long would you have?" asked Fairfield. "When would they notice you weren't back?"

"That depends on Mrs. Sill. Sometimes, she's in the kitchen when I bring in the wood."

Fairfield groaned. "That doesn't make it easy," he said. "Are they expecting you now?"

"I'm late for supper. They'll look for me quick as they finish eating," said Gregory.

"Then, let's go. It will soon snow. We might get to Harpers Ferry first, though. If we don't, they can track us."

"Dogs wouldn't need footprints," said Gregory.

"Does your master have a dog?"

"No, but the neighbors do," said Gregory. He took a last look at the house he had built.

"We'll leave the road about a mile from here." Fairfield started to move. "I found a shortcut."

"A lot of people may know me in Harpers Ferry," said Gregory.

"No, they won't. I've brought a disguise. Start thinking you're seventy-two and worn out."

"I feel that way already," said Gregory. "You can't make me look it, though."

"Oh yes, I can. Leave it to me. And stop thinking you're down-and-out. Other people are worse off than you."

They had walked almost a mile. The old bullet wound in Gregory's foot hurt him. The wind never stopped whistling. Still, they caught the sound of a wagon behind them. "Get off the road," said Fairfield. "Lie down in the ditch."

Gregory jumped down. He threw himself flat onto the cold mud. Fairfield walked slowly on. The wagon rumbled past. Then, it stopped. Gregory could make out the driver's words.

"You seen a tall, young slave passing?"

"I think I did," Fairfield answered.

"How long ago? Where did you see him?"

"It was a way back by that new house. This big, black man came running out of it. Practically bumped into me."

"He came this way?" asked Mr. Sill.

"He was going the other way when I saw him."

"Thought for sure he'd head for Harpers Ferry!" Mr. Sill turned his wagon, and it rumbled off.

Chapter 13

Baltimore Station

They stopped at a barn on the edge of Harpers Ferry. It felt good to get out of the wind. Fairfield went in as though he lived there. He must have made friends with the owner. Behind a haystack lay a package of clothes. On top were black trousers and a coat. Gregory started to undress.

"Wait," said Fairfield. "Let's do the top first."

"Top of what?" asked Gregory.

"Top of you. We have to shave it. You've got to be bald."

"Oh," said Gregory. He could see it was a good idea. Anyway, he'd never been vain about his hair.

Fairfield shaved all the top of his head. He left the back and sides as thick as ever. Then, he handed Gregory a small mirror.

"It looks queer," said Gregory, "but not old."

"Just wait, will you?" Fairfield reached for powder. In a minute he had turned Gregory's hair white. Then, carefully, he powdered his eyebrows.

Gregory looked in the mirror. He was impressed. Fairfield got out a beard next. It was mixed gray and white. It felt prickly.

"You're a new man," said Fairfield. "Do you need a mustache?" Gregory thought he did. It took them a while to make it look right.

"Now, get dressed," said Fairfield. "We've got a train to catch." He threw off his coat and old hat. Underneath, Fairfield was well dressed. He pulled new boots and a cane out of the hay. Then, he grabbed a beaver hat and cloak.

"Now, I'm John Percy of Percy Manor, Richmond. Remember that. You're Nathaniel, my servant. You go everywhere I go. I can't get along without you. You're devoted to me. You bring me brandy and pills. You brush dust off my coat."

"I'll try," said Gregory. It wouldn't be easy. Nathaniel wasn't his type.

"Come on," said Fairfield. "Keep your hat off when you can. That bald head would fool your own mother."

It was snowing outside the barn. Gregory left his hat off. The snow fell on his bald head.

"No use catching pneumonia," Fairfield said. "Wear the hat till we get to the station."

Soon, they were in the center of Harpers Ferry. Some faces looked familiar. No one knew Gregory, though. Their train was already in the station. Fairfield bought tickets to Cleveland, Ohio. Then, they ran to their cars. Several heads turned to watch them. Gregory still had a slight limp from the wound to his foot. Even so, he moved fast to catch the train. Gregory got in the car for blacks. Fairfield ran forward. In Baltimore, they would meet and change trains.

"Uncle, you sure can run!" said a young man. He was sitting across the aisle. "I saw you just sprint along that platform. You weren't even out of breath. You're going to live to be a hundred."

Gregory groaned. "I don't know, son," he said.

In Baltimore, he remembered to hobble off the car. Mr. Fairfield stood on the platform. Together they walked to the northbound train. "There's your car," Fairfield said.

"Wait a minute," a conductor called. "You can't just take a slave into Pennsylvania. You've got to prove you're his owner."

"I already have the tickets," said Fairfield. "What do you take me for? A thief?"

"No, sir. It's the rule, though. Too many slaves escaping north. That's why. It's in your interest, sir. Better not argue."

"Where do I go to prove I'm the owner?"

"Ticket counter. They'll look at your papers."

Fairfield swore under his breath. Gregory sweated. Inside the door, he wanted to turn and run. Across the room stood Mrs. Rombey. She was waiting in line at the ticket counter.

He nudged Fairfield. "That's my old mistress. No, not Mrs. Sill. It's Rombey's wife."

"Pull yourself together. She won't know you," Fairfield grumbled. "In fact, guess what! She's going to get us on that train. What's her first name?"

"Amelia," said Gregory. "We always called her Miss Amelia."

Fairfield left Gregory at the end of the line. He walked to the counter. Then, he turned and started back. At that moment, he caught Mrs. Rombey's eye. He gasped. His mouth hung open. Then, a sweet smile broke over

his face. "Amelia! No, pardon me. I have to call you Mrs. Rombey now. How many years since we met?"

"Why, how do you do?" said Mrs. Rombey. She was clearly confused. "A right number of years, I guess."

"Far too many," said Fairfield. "I once thought I'd never see you again. 'Good-bye, John,' you said. Those words sounded so final."

"Did I say that?" Mrs. Rombey looked nervous.

"Oh, yes," said Fairfield. "But life is kind. Here I am, seeing you once more."

"I called you John, did I?" asked Mrs. Rombey.

"Have you forgotten? You let me call you Amelia, too. Then, one day you said, 'Good-bye, John.'"

"I suppose I was going away," said Mrs. Rombey.

"Alas, you were. And I went away, too. But here, of all places, we meet again."

"Well, I came here for a funeral," Mrs. Rombey said. "An uncle of mine."

"That's a sad reason," said Fairfield.

"Are you traveling with your family?" she asked.

Fairfield shook his head sadly. "Amelia, I have never married. I have no family. I have one servant." He signaled to Gregory to come. "This old man has been with me since I was a child. You remember Nathaniel? He is devoted to me."

Gregory swallowed hard. Mrs. Rombey looked him up and down.

"Well, he's the right sort to have," she said.

"Yes, he is. They're making trouble for me in this station, though. I never thought to bring papers. I can't prove he belongs to me."

"Absurd!" said Mrs. Rombey. "Well, I can speak for you. They know me. I believe they'll take my word."

"I'm sure they would," said Fairfield. "How could they doubt it? I'm sorry to trouble you."

Mrs. Rombey was enjoying herself. "Oh well, it's not much trouble."

The man behind the counter listened politely. He knew the lady's family. She said she had known Mr. John Percy for years.

"And you can swear the servant belongs to him?"

Yes, she had known the old man for years, too. Gregory smiled and nodded. The ticket man was satisfied. Fairfield had time to make a low bow. He told Mrs. Rombey he would never forget. Then, they hurried to their train.

Chapter 14

Storm on Lake Erie

They got to Cleveland early in the morning. Ice glittered on the puddles. They could see their breath in the raw air.

"It's still January," said Fairfield. "This is normal weather here."

"Won't the lake be frozen?" asked Gregory.

"No," said Fairfield. "It won't be. Don't worry. Just act like an old man. Ohio is free, but you can run into slave-catchers. They've got federal law on their side, too."

"Mr. Sill hasn't had time to advertise me," said Gregory.

"Don't be too sure. We've had time to get here. He's had time to send word you're gone."

They walked from the station to the port. The sun had come up. The lake was bright blue.

"That's your boat," said Fairfield. He pointed to a small steamer. Its name was the *Philadelphia*. "I'll take you to meet the captain. Then, I'll be off. You won't need me any longer."

"You're not going to Canada?" asked Gregory.

"No, the captain will carry you to Canada. You couldn't pay me to take a boat. I get seasick if I ruffle my bathwater."

The sailor on guard let them board the *Philadelphia*. Fairfield looked uncomfortable.

"I can't stay," he said. "Would you call your captain?"

Romulus came at once. "Hello, Fairfield," he said. "How was your trip? Say, you don't mean this is Gregory!" Romulus laughed out loud. "Excuse me," he said. "You look kind of old to be a heartbreaker. Would you mind taking that beard off?"

"Is it safe?" asked Fairfield.

"He's safe on my ship," said Romulus. Gregory took his beard and hat off. "That's more like it," the captain said.

"I'm going now," said Fairfield. "Good-bye." He was in such a hurry, Gregory hardly had time to thank him.

"Won't you rest a little?" asked Romulus. "You look kind of sick."

"Water's too rough," said Fairfield. "I'll be fine on dry land."

"Make yourself at home, Gregory," Romulus said. "I've got four other fugitives on board. I'll introduce you."

"How big is your crew?" asked Gregory.

"There are five of us, too. This is a small freighter. Everyone on board is black and an abolitionist."

They left port an hour later. Soon, the day got warmer. The sky was bright. Not for months had Gregory felt so good. He had the run of the boat. He strolled. He sat, talking, on coiled ropes. He went below deck to admire the engine. When he came up, the sky had turned cloudy. The boat went into port at Toledo. Romulus told them to get below. "No use advertising yourselves," he said. It began to rain, so no one minded.

Then, a sailor's voice said, "There's a United States marshal wants aboard, sir."

"A marshal!" Romulus groaned. "What does he want?"

"He won't say. He's got some deputies with him."

"Go tell our passengers to hide," said Romulus.

"I'm going," Gregory called softly. "I'll tell the others."

Romulus's head showed in the hatchway. "The safest place is above the boiler. Can't get more than two up there, though."

Gregory told the runaways to find hiding places. It wouldn't be easy for five.

"Two of you better come to the boiler room," said Gregory. There was a sort of shelf there, above the tank. Gregory helped the others climb up. Then, he went back to the hold. Everyone was out of sight. He could hear Romulus's voice above.

"You're wasting your time, marshal. You're wasting mine, too. What makes you think I'm carrying fugitives from justice?"

"I said fugitive slaves, captain. You heard me perfectly. I've had complaints about your boat before. So, this time, I got a search warrant."

Romulus sighed. "Well, go ahead. I just wish you'd picked a time it wasn't storming."

"You call this little rain a storm?"

"Can't you feel that wind coming up? It's going to rage in twenty minutes."

In a corner of the hold, Gregory found a trunk. He got into it and let the top close. Then, he wondered if he would smother. He heard feet coming down the ladder. Breathless, he waited for someone to open the trunk. Then, he realized the feet were gone. All he heard was wind.

He pushed the top up again. The hold was almost dark. He got quietly out of the trunk. Now, the boat was rolling so, he could hardly walk. He stumbled to the ladder. He heard voices.

"We're way out in the lake," the marshal was saying. "You fools have let the boat drift."

"It's the storm," said Romulus. "The wind cut us loose. I can't do anything about it."

"You've *got* to do something. Get us back to port."

"That won't be easy, marshal. We might get blown against the rocks."

"I think you made the boat drift," said the marshal. "You saw me go in your cabin. You knew the two fugitives were there."

"So then, I decided to commit suicide," said Romulus. "I cut the boat loose in the storm."

"I'm not saying why you did it. I'm saying you'll get into trouble."

"I'm already in it," said Romulus. "We can't get the engine going. Maybe we can just ride out the storm. I don't know. One thing I promise you. You and your deputies can take the first lifeboat. You can make it back to shore from here. Of course if we drift out much further—"

"Why aren't you working on that engine?" the marshal yelled.

"I was when you sent for me. I'll get back there now."

Gregory dropped from the ladder. Then, Romulus came down in the hold. He went straight to the engine room. Soon, the pistons began making queer noises. The engine didn't really start, though. Gregory sighed.

Romulus came out of the engine room and went up the ladder.

"Isn't there any hope?" the marshal asked.

"Not today, I'm afraid. I'll probably need a new boiler," said Romulus.

"Are you sure it's safe to go in one of those lifeboats?"

Gregory waited. For a time, he heard only the wind. Then came a creaking noise and shouts. They must be lowering one of the boats, he thought. A minute later, the hatch opened.

"You can come up now," Romulus called. "The marshal's gone. Two of his deputies are really good rowers."

"Will they make it?" Gregory asked.

"Of course they will. And we'll make a beeline for Detroit," said Romulus.

"How can we get there without an engine?"

"I guess the engine will work now," said Romulus. "It's a funny thing. Somebody took out a little valve by mistake. I found it a minute ago. It's already screwed back in. Queer how it happened."

"Very queer," said Gregory. "Did the marshal take those two fugitives he found?"

"No. I told him they'd make the lifeboat too heavy."

The storm howled all the way to Detroit. The passengers had to bail out water. But no one minded.

Detroit looked beautiful. It was free and on solid land. Romulus advised everyone to stay on board. "You're on your own in town," he said. "It's a big risk."

Gregory nodded. He knew it was true. He went down the gangplank, even so.

Chapter 15

One Way to Canada

It seemed to Becky that they should have arrived. Romulus had been gone 10 days. Sometimes, she was on top of the world. She thought Gregory would be there any minute. Other times, she knew he wouldn't. The storm was the worst she had seen in Canada. You could hardly stand up in the wind. How could Barbara go around with a smile? Her husband was out in it. So was Gregory.

But the storm passed. No one spoke of any boats going down. No one brought good news, either. Even Barbara began to look worried. Then, one morning, the *Philadelphia* chugged into port. Romulus came at once to find Becky. He looked glum.

"What happened to him? Did he get arrested?" she asked.

"I don't think so," said Romulus. "We got to Detroit, all right. I had five fugitives on board. Three of them just had to see the town. Gregory was the first to leave. His master had him advertised. In fact, he had agents in town, looking for him. They heard the *Philadelphia* was in port. Pretty soon, they got a marshal to come. We just barely saved our last two fugitives. We lowered them in barrels onto the dock. That marshal really combed the boat. Then, he left deputies on the pier to watch. It was a problem getting the barrels back on board."

"I sent a man to find Gregory in town. That was impossible. We waited two days more. Gregory never came back to the boat. He's hiding in Detroit. At least, I think so."

"How will he ever get away?" asked Becky.

"He was disguised as an old slave, Nathaniel. He left the clothes and beard on board, though. He may have to wait three months. I guess they can't watch the port forever."

Becky shook her head. "You don't know if the marshal caught him. Why do we just sit here?"

"Because there's nothing else we can do," said Romulus. Then, he went home to his wife.

Hamilton came to see her the next day. He had been to Detroit again. "Don't set your heart on any fugitive, honey. They are always running," he said. "I was sitting, talking to this Gregory. He came into the Erie Tavern one night. It was snowing. I said 'Sit down here, man.' Then we talked. Across from us sat a real stool pigeon. Wouldn't look you in the eye. He kept listening, though. And Gregory talked too much. He mentioned Harpers Ferry. He said he was a carpenter. Kind of a fool, if you ask me. Anyway, the stool pigeon took a last, close look at him. Then, he went out the door. I asked Gregory if he knew the man. He didn't, but the pigeon knew him, all right. A few minutes later, the waiter came rushing in. He told Gregory to leave by the back door. Gregory just got out when a marshal arrived."

"So he got away?" Becky asked. "Do you know where he went?"

"Yes, I have a pretty good idea. He got away that time. They'll catch him yet, though. The man's worth too much."

"You said you know where this Gregory is hiding, Hamilton. Where? Is it safe?"

"Sure," he said. "Harper, the waiter I mentioned, has a house. His wife takes in boarders. Sometimes they're runaways. She doesn't even make them pay. He'll be all right if he stays there. Let's talk about something else, shall we?"

Becky tried to talk about other things for 10 minutes. Then, she said they needed her in the kitchen. She wanted to think. It didn't take her long to make a plan. After work, she walked to Barbara's house. Romulus was sitting by the fire. Becky didn't really want him to hear, but she couldn't say so.

"You still got that disguise of Gregory's?" she asked him.

"You mean the black suit? It's still on the boat. And the beard is, too. Why do you ask?"

"Well, that's what I came to tell Barbara. It won't interest you much, Romulus."

He frowned. "You got some crazy notion. I can see that. Go ahead and talk. I'm interested."

Barbara laughed. "Don't let him scare you, Becky. Just go ahead and tell me."

"You didn't see me arrive in Canada," said Becky. "I was disguised as a rich lady. I still have the beautiful silk dress I wore. I have a bonnet, too, with a veil. I'm going to put them on again, on the way to Detroit. I'll take Gregory his disguise. We can come back on the ferry."

Romulus groaned. "I knew it! I knew you'd think of something wild. Want to get yourself arrested?"

"I won't get caught," Becky promised. "No one will see I'm black."

"In the first place, you don't know where Gregory is."

"Yes, I do. At least, I think he's at the waiter Harper's house."

"Well, if he is, I'd better get him myself." Romulus sounded tired and hopeless.

"No," said Becky. "You may be free. But everybody knows you help fugitive slaves. In fact, there must be a warrant out for your arrest. I hear you had trouble with a U.S. marshal."

Romulus nodded. "Just a small difference of opinion. They may want to question me, though. You've got a point. The trouble is, you're a woman. You can pass for white all right. If you owned slaves, though, you'd travel with your maid. You wouldn't go around with an old man."

"She can find some reason for it," said Barbara. "She's right, Romulus. She'll do this better than you. Better give her Gregory's disguise."

"Yes, please," said Becky. "I get paid tomorrow. I'll be able to buy ferry tickets."

The hotel gave her the day off without arguing. She left at six in the morning. She carried her dress with Gregory's things in a bag. At the dock, she bought her round-trip ticket.

On the ferry, she found a small, empty room. Shut inside, she changed into her disguise. Then, she walked out, a rich lady.

On the dock, she stopped a black worker. "Do you know Mrs. Harper's boarding house?" she asked.

"Sure do, ma'am," he answered. Then, he acted suspicious. "Are you looking for someone?"

"I used to know Mrs. Harper," she said. "I'd like to call on her."

The man nodded. He told her where to find the house. It was a long way from the port. Morning was half gone when she got there. She rang the bell. A black woman opened the door.

"Are you Mrs. Harper?" asked Becky. "I'm looking for Gregory. He's here, isn't he?"

"We haven't any Gregory here, ma'am."

"Please don't call me ma'am. I'm Gregory's friend. I have to find him. I've come to take him to Ontario."

Mrs. Harper stared at her. Then, she shook her head. "There's some mistake, ma'am."

"May I come in?" Becky asked.

"No, ma'am. I'm sorry. I don't allow strangers."

"Mrs. Harper," Becky said, "*you're* making a mistake. Not me."

The woman shook her head again.

"I'll leave a message for Gregory, then," Becky told her. "Tell him a friend of Romulus came. Give him this bundle of clothes. Tell him I'm waiting for Nathaniel on the dock."

Mrs. Harper said nothing. She took the clothes and shut the door. Becky wanted to scream for Gregory. Yet she couldn't be sure he was there. Maybe Mrs. Harper really didn't know him. The only thing to do was return to the dock.

She started back without much hope. How long should she wait? Would people ask her questions?

She stopped at the end of the pier to think. Soon, there was a clatter of feet. An old man came running up behind her. Even though he limped, he was mighty quick for his years.

"Are you looking for me, ma'am?" he asked. "I'm Nathaniel."

Becky nodded. She couldn't find words.

"How did you know where I was?" he asked. The ferry whistled loudly. They must hurry.

"Wait," said Becky. She almost ran to the ticket office. "One way to Canada." she said. She paid and walked out again.

"All ready, Nathaniel?" she asked. She gave him the ticket. "You're going to grow young again in a new land."

He held his breath a moment. Then, he whispered, "Becky?"

"Don't play guessing games," she said. "We have a ferry to catch."

He laughed. He could have sung. Only there was a crowd around him. The old risk was still there. He hobbled behind her up the gangplank. Then, the whistle sounded again. They stood silent, as the gangplank lifted. Swiftly, the boat moved out into the river.

"We're in Canadian waters," Becky said.

He couldn't wait any longer. He grabbed her in his arms, and kissed her, veil and all.